This edition published by Parragon Inc. 2013

Parragon Inc.
440 Park Avenue South, 13th Floor
New York, NY 10016
www.parragon.com

Edited by Gemma Louise Lowe
Designed by Pete Hampshire
Production by Charlene Vaughan

ISBN 978-1-4723-2017-9

Printed in China

Little Red Riding Minnie

PaRragon

Bath • New York • Singapore • Hong Kong • Cologne • Delhi
Melbourne • Amsterdam • Johannesburg • Shenzhen

Once upon a time, there was a kindhearted girl who was loved by all who knew her. Her grandmother had made her a cape of red wool as a gift. The girl wore it so often that her family, and friends began to call her Little Red Riding Minnie.

One day, Little Red Riding Minnie learned that her grandmother was sick with a bad cold. She decided to bake a batch of her famous oatmeal-chocolate-chip cookies. Those were sure to make her grandmother feel better!

After the cookies had cooled, Little Red Riding Minnie put them in a cookie tin. Then she packed some super-strong menthol cough drops into another cookie tin. She thought her grandmother could probably use some of those, too.

Little Red Riding Minnie put both cookie tins into her basket and set off for her grandmother's house.

The route to her grandmother's house took Little Red Riding
Minnie through the center of town—straight down Main Street,
which was a very busy shopping area.

Little Red Riding Minnie loved saying hello to all the shopkeepers
as she passed their shops. She was enjoying her walk very much.
Then, just as she passed the post office, Big Bad Pete jumped out
of an alleyway and blocked her path!

"Hello, Red," he said with a smirk. "And where might you be going with that big basket?"

Now, Big Bad Pete was known to everyone around town as a scoundrel. He was certainly the last person Little Red Riding Minnie would have wanted to meet on her way to her grandmother's house. But Little Red Riding Minnie tried to be polite to everyone and that included Big Bad Pete!

"Well, if you must know," Little Red Riding Minnie replied, hugging her basket tightly, "I'm taking some of my famous oatmeal-chocolate-chip cookies to my grandmother. She has a terrible cold. Now, if you'll excuse me…."

And with that, Little Red Riding Minnie hurried away.

As Big Bad Pete watched her go, his mouth began to water. Little Red Riding Minnie's oatmeal-chocolate-chip cookies were famous—famously delicious!

Big Bad Pete had to get his hands on those cookies, even if it meant tricking Little Red Riding Minnie.

So, while Little Red Riding Minnie continued along Main Street, stopping to window-shop here, and talk to shopkeepers there, Big Bad Pete ducked down an alleyway, raced along the backstreets, and zipped through some backyards.

Big Bad Pete arrived at Little Red Riding Minnie's grandmother's house first. He knew he had to come up with a plan.

As he hurried up the front path, Big Bad Pete spotted the grandmother's laundry hanging out to dry on the clothes line in the yard.

"Hmmm…," he said as he came up with a crafty plan to get the cookies.

Big Bad Pete grabbed the grandmother's clean clothing, and hid behind the house. He would be ready for Little Red Riding Minnie when she arrived!

Minutes later, Little Red Riding Minnie skipped up the garden path toward her grandmother's front door. She was singing happily to herself, and didn't notice anything unusual.

Before she could knock, Big Bad Pete jumped out from behind a bush. He was disguised in her grandmother's clothing!

"Oh, hello, Little Red Riding Minnie," Big Bad Pete squeaked, trying to sound like her grandmother. "Have you come to pay your grandmother a visit?"

"Why … uh … yes," Little Red Riding Minnie stammered. Grandmother's cold must be very bad, indeed, she thought. She looks awful, and I have never heard her sound so squeaky!

Little Red Riding Minnie looked more closely at her grandmother, and started to notice some peculiar things. Something was definitely not right!

"Grandmother," Little Red Riding Minnie said, "what big ears you have!"

"All the better to hear you with, my dear," Big Bad Pete replied in his best grandmother voice.

"And what big eyes you have!" Little Red Riding Minnie exclaimed.

Big Bad Pete crept closer to her. "All the better to see you with, my dear," he squeaked.

"And what big teeth you have!"
Little Red Riding Minnie continued.

Big Bad Pete moved even closer.
Now he was right over her. "All the
better to eat your famous oatmeal-
chocolate-chip cookies with, my
dear!" he shouted.

And with that, Big Bad Pete
snatched a cookie tin out of Little
Red Riding Minnie's basket, threw
off his disguise and began to
laugh wickedly.

"Ah-ha-ha-ha! I tricked you! Now your cookies are all mine!"

As Little Red Riding Minnie watched, Big Bad Pete pulled off the cover of the cookie tin, threw his head back, and emptied the entire contents into his mouth. Unfortunately for Big Bad Pete … it was the wrong tin.

It took only a few seconds before the super-strong menthol cough drops began to work their magic. Big Bad Pete's face turned bright pink and his eyes became very large. He ran down the garden path, and away from Little Red Riding Minnie. He needed to find a drink of water!

Just then, Little Red Riding Minnie's real grandmother opened the door.

"Oh, hello, dear," she said as she dabbed at her nose with a handkerchief. "Is everything all right?"

"Oh, yes, Grandmother,"
Little Red Riding Minnie replied.
"Everything is just fine."

So, Little Red Riding
Minnie had a very
pleasant visit with her
ill grandmother, who
was feeling much better
because she had enjoyed
the oatmeal-chocolate-chip
cookies so much.

Little Red Riding
Minnie left the recipe
with her grandmother, and
walked home, stopping to
say hello to some friends
along the way.

Meanwhile, Big Bad Pete decided that Little Red Riding Minnie's cookies were not all they were cracked up to be. As he drank bucket after bucket of water, he vowed never to trick anyone for their famously delicious cookies ever again.